GHOUL SCHOOL RULES!

GHOUL SCHOOL
RULES!

BY MICHELLE POPLOFF
ILLUSTRATED BY BILL BASSO

SCHOLASTIC INC.

New York   Toronto   London   Auckland   Sydney

Mexico City   New Delhi   Hong Kong   Buenos Aires

For Gina, Lucille, and Kimberly:
Wanda's "fang-tastic" fairy godmothers!
—M. P.

For all of my godchildren
—Godfather B. B.

No part of this publication may be reproduced in whole or in part, or stored in a retrieval system, or transmitted in any form or by any means, electronic, mechanical, photocopying, recording, or otherwise, without written permission of the publisher. For information regarding permission, write to Scholastic Inc., Attention: Permissions Department, 555 Broadway, New York, NY 10012.

ISBN 0-439-16453-2

Text copyright © 2001 by Michelle Poploff.
Illustrations copyright © 2001 by Bill Basso.
All rights reserved.   Published by Scholastic Inc.
SCHOLASTIC, LITTLE APPLE PAPERBACKS, and associated logos
are trademarks and/or registered trademarks of Scholastic Inc.

12 11 10 9 8 7 6 5 4 3 2   3 4 5 6/0
                                           40

Printed in the U.S.A.
First Scholastic printing, September 2001

CONTENTS

Chapter 1
FIRST-DAY JITTERS

"Rise and shine, dearie! Today is the big day," called Granny Doomsday.

Wanda Doomsday pulled the covers over her head.

Today was the day, all right.

The dreadful, awful first day of school.

Wanda groaned.

Maybe I'll tell Granny I'm sick, she thought.

Her stomach *did* feel sort of slippery-flippery.

"Wanda! Wanda Lucille!" Granny
called. "Did you hear me?"

"Yes, Granny," Wanda called back. She
reached for her new birthday watch.

Tick, tick, tick.

Wanda wondered why time goes so
quickly over the summer and so slowly
during school.

She yawned and stretched.

She *was* looking forward to wearing
her new witch watch to school.

Besides, Wanda thought, *Granny will
know I'm faking.*

She quickly got dressed.

She poufed up her hair, puffed out her
cape, and went downstairs for breakfast.

Granny handed Wanda her new lunch box.
"There's a special treat inside," she said.
"Wait until lunchtime to open it."
"Speaking of time," said Wanda's
brother, Artie, "we should leave now."
"Won't you be lonely without us,
Granny?" Wanda asked in a small voice.

10

Granny Doomsday hugged Wanda.
"Seems to me that you need a spooky
back-to-school riddle to get you going,"
she said.
She tapped her pointy chin for a moment.
"What time is it when ten ghosts chase
after one goblin?"

11

"Ten after one!" shouted Wanda.

"That's my ghoul—er—girl," said Granny. She hugged Artie and Wanda and checked her watch.

"I'll see you at three o'clock."

Wanda looked at her witch watch.

"That's not for another seven big, fat hours," she wailed.

Granny whispered in Wanda's ear.

"Why did the witch wear her watch when she was out on her broom?"

"Why?" Wanda asked.

"Simple," said Granny. "She wanted to see time fly."

"Oh, Granny," Wanda groaned.

Granny winked.

"Trust me, dearie. You'll be so busy at school that time will fly for you, too."

Chapter 2
GHOUL-DILOCKS

When the Doomsdays were near
the school, Artie ran ahead to catch
up with a friend.

Wanda kicked at a stone as she
walked alone.

Then, suddenly, she felt a push from
behind.

"Hey, Ghoul-dilocks, aren't you a little
early for Halloween?"

That loud, scratchy voice made
Wanda itchy.

It was Wayne the Pain Dobbs.

"Maybe Ghoul-dilocks thinks she's

going to ghoul school," said Wayne's pal
Hector.

Wanda whirled around and poked Wayne
in the chest. "For your information I *am*
going to ghoul school. And listen up—
the girls in ghoul school rule!"
Wanda flicked her cape in their faces.
"Oh, you are way scary, Wanda," said
Wayne, pretending to shake.
The boys followed behind her.
"Where did you go for summer vacation?"
asked Hector. "Witch-ita, Kansas?"
Wanda spun around again.
"All right, hotshots, what's a witch's
favorite subject?"
The boys stopped in their tracks.
"Spelling," Wanda said in her deepest,
scariest voice. "And don't you forget it.
I'm the best at casting spells."

Wayne and Hector stood with their mouths hanging open.

Wanda walked away.

They didn't follow her this time.

She hoped those two weren't in her class.

Last year she had Mrs. Bono, the best teacher in the whole school.

If only it were last year again, Wanda thought.

"Good morning, Wanda," said a kind voice.

It was Mrs. Bono.

"I have good news. I'm going to be your teacher again," she said, smiling.

Wanda jumped up and down.

"That is so awesome, Mrs. Bono!"

She couldn't wait to tell her good friend Helen Hooper.

Wanda looked around for Helen.
Instead she saw Wayne and Hector
lining up for Mrs. Bono's class.
Wanda felt like she was going to be sick.
No faking this time.

Chapter 3
DOUBLE DOOM

"The first thing we are going to do
this year is sit in alphabetical order
by last names," said Mrs. Bono.
She held up a big blue box.
"If anyone has other seating suggestions,
please put a note in here."
Mrs. Bono began calling out her
students' names.
"Wanda," she said, "you can sit right
there next to Wayne."
Wayne the Pain Dobbs looked worried.
Wanda Doomsday felt doomed.

"I have a surprise, class," announced Mrs. Bono. "We're going to kick off the school year with Fall Field Day. Each grade will be divided into two teams. Our class will be the gold team and Mrs. Zolt's class will be blue."

"What will we be doing?" asked Buffy Gotrocks.

"We'll have relay races, volleyball, a hula hoop contest, and a tug-of-war," Mrs. Bono answered. "We'll practice all week. Your families can come and cheer for you on Friday."

Wanda loved hula hoops and running. She wiggled happily in her seat.

Mrs. Bono's class began practicing
outside right away.
They stepped into potato sacks and
hopped till they dropped.
Wanda twisted and turned with a
hula hoop.
"Wanda and Wayne," said Mrs. Bono,
"get ready to practice for the three-
legged race."
She tied Wanda's right leg to Wayne's
left leg.
"Put your arms around each other's waist
for balance," she said.
"No way!" Wanda and Wayne said
together.
"Remember," said Mrs. Bono patiently,
"teamwork is what Field Day is all
about."

When everyone was ready, Mrs. Bono
called out, "On your mark! Get set!
Go!"

Wanda and Wayne wobbled and hobbled
a few steps, then fell down.

"*Ooph!* Get off of me, Wanda!" Wayne
yelled.

"You tripped me!" said Wanda.

Mrs. Bono ran over to help.

"All you need is more practice," she said. "We still have a few days."

"I don't think I can stand a few more days of this," said Wayne.

My thoughts exactly, thought Wanda.

27

Chapter 4
DREAM TEAM TROUBLES

The next day, the gold team divided up
for volleyball practice.

When it was Wanda's turn to serve,
she couldn't get the ball over the net.

"No fair! Do-over! The sun was
in my eyes!" Wanda said, stamping
her foot.

"No do-overs, Wanda," said Buffy.

"It's our turn to serve."

Buffy served the ball over the net.

Wayne slapped it back.

Helen hit it over toward Wanda.

"I've got it, I've got it! This one is
mine!" Wanda shouted.

She stepped back to get the ball and
bumped heads with Wayne.

The ball hit the ground.

"Well, I almost had it," Wanda said.
"Are you sure this is supposed to be fun,
Mrs. Bono?" she asked. "This Field Day
stuff is harder than homework."
Mrs. Bono just smiled.

Later, Wanda opened her lunch box as
she sat with Helen.
"Look, Helen! Granny packed both of
us her great batty brownies."
"Yum! Thanks!" said Helen.

"And Granny sent a riddle," said
Wanda. "Why didn't the skeleton go to
the school dance?"

"Whympf?" asked Helen, her mouth
filled with brownie.

"He had no *body* to go with," said
Wanda.

Helen laughed.

"After lunch I'm putting a note in our
class suggestion box," she said. "I'm
suggesting that we don't get homework
one Friday out of every month."

Wanda twirled a bright orange curl.

"You just gave me a neat idea, Helen.
I'm going to suggest that we change
seats once a month. It would be fun to
sit next to different people."

Helen agreed.

"You could suggest we sit in alphabetical order by first name."

"That's an awful idea, Helen," Wanda said. "I'd be stuck next to Wayne the Pain again."

Helen ate the last bite of Granny's batty brownie.

"I've got it!" she cried. "Let's sit according to our middle names. Mine's Mary."

"Mine is Lucille," said Wanda.

"L and M are just one letter apart." She jumped up from the table.

"I'm putting that idea in the suggestion box right away!"

Chapter 5
GO! GO! GOLD TEAM!

Finally, Field Day Friday arrived.
Principal Shaw welcomed the teams and
explained the rules.
Wanda couldn't wait to get started.
She waved to Granny in the stands.
Granny waved back with both hands.
At last, the games began.
The blue team won the relay race after
Buffy dropped the baton.
Next, Wayne helped bring home the
gold for the tug-of-war.

Wanda came in first place for her team
in the hula hoop competition.
Granny whooped from the sidelines.
During the volleyball game, the score
was tied.
Wanda saw the ball coming her way.
This is my big chance! she thought.
Wanda didn't know Buffy was thinking
the same thing.

Wanda stepped to the side and smashed
into Buffy as they both went for the ball.
"That ball was mine!" Buffy yelled at
Wanda. "You just had to hog it. Now
you've lost the game for the gold team."
Wanda felt awful.
She had let her team down.
She didn't even want to be in the three-
legged race.

"Come on, Wanda, we've been practicing all week," said Wayne.

"I'll just make us lose again," said Wanda.

Wayne thought for a moment.

"Knock, knock," he said.

Wanda sighed.

"Who's there?" she asked.

"Police."

"Police who?"

"Police be my partner?" said Wayne.

Wanda couldn't help laughing.

"Oh, all right," she said.

Mrs. Bono tied their legs together and wished them luck.

"You can do it," she said. "Ready? Steady? Go!"

The whistle blew and Wayne and

Wanda were off.

Wanda kept her eyes straight ahead.
She could hear Wayne huffing and
chuffing beside her.

Then, out of the corner of her eye,
she saw Ronni and Joey from Mrs. Zolt's
class.
They were getting closer and closer.
Now they were a step ahead.
Then two steps.
"Come on, Bat Girl," huffed Wayne.
"Let's fly."
That was all Wanda needed to hear.
She took a deep breath and pushed
forward.

Two more long steps and they were past
the other kids.

Then, with a final push, they tumbled
over the finish line to take first place.

Wayne and Wanda sat up and slapped
high fives.

"We did it, partner!" laughed Wanda.

Wayne tugged on Wanda's muddy curls.

"Yeah, Moldy-locks," he said with a grin.

They tried to get up and fell down again.

"Hey!" yelled Wayne. "Someone untie us!"

Chapter 6
WHAT'S THE BIG IDEA?

At the end of the day, Wanda and Helen
walked home together.

Their gold-medal badges flashed in the
sun.

"It's Friday and we didn't get homework
today," said Helen. "Maybe Mrs. Bono
read my suggestion."

"I hope she reads mine," said Wanda.
"Then maybe we can sit together next
month."

At the stoplight, the girls caught up to
Wayne.

"Hey, Wayne," said Wanda, "what's your middle name?"

"It's Louis," said Wayne. "Wayne Louis Dobbs."

The light changed to green.

Wayne walked across the street.

Wanda and Helen stood still.

They looked at each other.

"Wayne Louis Dobbs?" shouted Wanda.

"Wanda Lucille Doomsday. Both of our initials are WLD. I'm doomed! I'll have to take my suggestion back first thing Monday morning."

"What will you tell Mrs. Bono?" asked Helen.

"I'll say I have a better suggestion."

Wanda snapped her fingers.

"I know!" she said. "I'll suggest that we sit next to kids born in the same month. How's that?"

"That depends," said Helen. "When's Wayne's birthday?"

Wanda clapped her hand to her head.

"There's only one way to find out. Come on, Helen."

When the light turned green again, the girls ran across the street.

"Hey, Wayne!" they called. "Wait up!"